Bagel was born to a loving mother Sadie who had 7 puppy beagles. Her dad Rusty is so proud of his family. They all live on a big farm in Arkansas.

Bagel is the rascal one of the litter. She has big dreams and she often sits alone to dream. She also likes to play with her brothers and sisters.

Her siblings think she is a dreamer! She often fantasizes about what is outside of the farm. She likes to run around and explore all the way to the fence at the edge of the farm.

One day Bagel meets an old mutt who has lived on the road his entire life. The old dog tells Bagel about the blue ocean! From that day on Bagel only talks about the blue ocean filled with whales blowing water, surfing dolphins, pelicans and seals. Bagel's new dream is to be friends with all of them.

Rusty tells Bagel he has never heard such nonsense.... "A lake you can swim in as large as the eye reaches"....nonsense! "Deep blue and not normal muddy brown water?"...such dreams - nonsense!

When Bagel tells Sadie, she gets scared and frightened that Bagel will get hurt. She wants Bagel to forget her dreams, stay at home and focus on her school work, chores and become a good hunting dog like her dad.

Bagel asks everyone she meets about the blue ocean and the dolphins. No one has ever heard of it. Not the cows, nor the fox, or the horse and even the gossipy hen. Bagel knows in her heart that the ocean is real. Every night when she goes to bed she dreams of the ocean.

Bagel becomes really sad. She begins to sit and stare down the long dusty road. One day she makes a big bold decision. She will show everyone they are wrong!! The ocean really exist and she will find it.

The next morning Bagel wakes up before the cock-a-doodle-doos and packs her bag with her favorite toy and some snacks because she is scared to get hungry on her journey.She looks at her family and whispers goodbye and cries because she doesn't know when she will see them again.

Then she heads down the long dusty road, with her tiny little bag and her heart full of adventure.

Bagel get to a crossroad but which way to the ocean? She is about to give up but then an old truck stops. On the back of the truck is an old dog. The old dog asks if she is lost. Bagel says she is looking for the way to the ocean. The old dog does not know where that is, but they are going to the city to sell apples. The old dog tells Bagel she can come if she promises not to eat any of the apples.

They arrive at the market in the city and Bagel has never seen so many people and animals before! It is loud and everyone is talking and shouting. The noise is unbearable for Bagel because she has such big ears so Bagel gets scared and runs toward the exit.

By the door she meets a kitten. She is crying because she cannot find her mommy. They were going to Oklahoma by bus but the kitten got lost from her mother in the crowd. Bagel does not know what a bus is but promises to help. Bagel lifts the kitten up on her back and starts to run around the market and suddenly the kitten shouts "there it is"!!

The little kitten is so happy to see her mommy again. The mommy cat invites Bagel to join them on the bus to Oklahoma. Bagel is very happy and begins to tell them about the ocean. In fact Bagel only talks about the ocean for the entire trip while the cat and kitten fall asleep.

The next morning, Bagel and the cats arrive at the bus station. They say goodbye to each other, and Bagel begins to ask the other animals at the bus station for directions. Neither Fred friendly rat nor Pierre the slow pigeon have heard of the ocean.

Suddenly Bagel hears a growling and turns around to see a gang of pit bulls. They ask if she is looking for trouble. Bagel says "No!" She ain't lookin' for trouble! "I am looking for the ocean." The pit bulls laugh at Bagel and offers her a ride to Austin because they are going to a biker rally with folks from all over the country who might have heard of it.

Bagel rides with the wild bunch through Texas. She sees longhorns and cowboys along the way. Her big ears flap as she is trying to hold on to the motorcycle. It is very scary but she feels free and adventurous.

Bagel arrives in Austin. The biker gang wants to get some BBQ and soda pop. Bagel has never had a soda pop and decides she doesn't like the bubbles in her nose.

Politely she thanks the pit bulls for the ride and heads out into Austin...but she does not know where to go. She is lost again.

Bagel walk down the street. She is all alone again. She is lost. Then she hears a hammer from a blacksmith and walks toward the sound. Inside she meets a mustang that introduces herself as Sally. Sally is admiring her new shoes. "Oh look at my shoes...so shiny, so stylish, so fast"

Bagel asks Sally if she has seen the ocean. Sally replies "No, but there is a really big river called the Colorado River. This river might take you to the ocean but it is a long way from Austin." Sally decides she can take Bagel to it and at the same time test out her new shoes.

Bagel and Sally begin to run out of the city to the prairie, but Bagel becomes so tired her little paws can't keep up with Sally. So, Sally offers her a ride on her back. They ride all day and Bagel holds onto Sally like her life depends on it. Poor Bagel becomes a little horseback sick.

Bagel is really tired in the evening. She falls fast asleep under the stars, close to Sally and close to the fire to keep her warm. Suddenly she hears someone whispering out in the darkness. Bagel uses her sharp ears and sharp eyes to discover it is a couple of coyotes sneaking in on their camp. They want to steal their food and Sally's shiny new shoes.

Bagel howls at the coyote and Sally wakes up to chase the coyotes away. Sally is so grateful that Bagel discovered the danger, and she appoints Bagel their official watchdog to keep them safe at night. Bagel is very proud, but she is also very sleepy. Duty comes before sleep. She sits by the campfire and listens to the night while Sally sleeps. Sally snores so much that Bagel could not sleep anyway.

The sun rises in the east and they get ready to ride. Bagel is so tired from keeping watch all night and falls asleep over Sally's back as they ride through New Mexico. Bagel thinks that is a strange name for a state. If this is New Mexico then where is Old Mexico? So Confusing.

Evening comes and it is time to camp again. Bagel gets ready to keep her watch. Sally snores again so loud that the ground shakes, so Bagel sneaks away from the camp because her big ears hurt from all that noise.

Bagel watches the stars and thinks of her family. She becomes sad and cries a little because she misses them. Suddenly she hears a raspy voice asking her why she is crying. Bagel looks down and sees a friendly old rattlesnake.

The rattlesnake introduces himself as Chappy. Bagel can see that Chappy is very old and wise. He tells her she can always go home, so there is no need for crying. He explains that Bagel's parents gave her four paws to explore, two ears to listen and one mouth to ask for advice. All animals look different but they have the same dreams. They will help if she asks for it and Bagel should follow her dream to become happy.

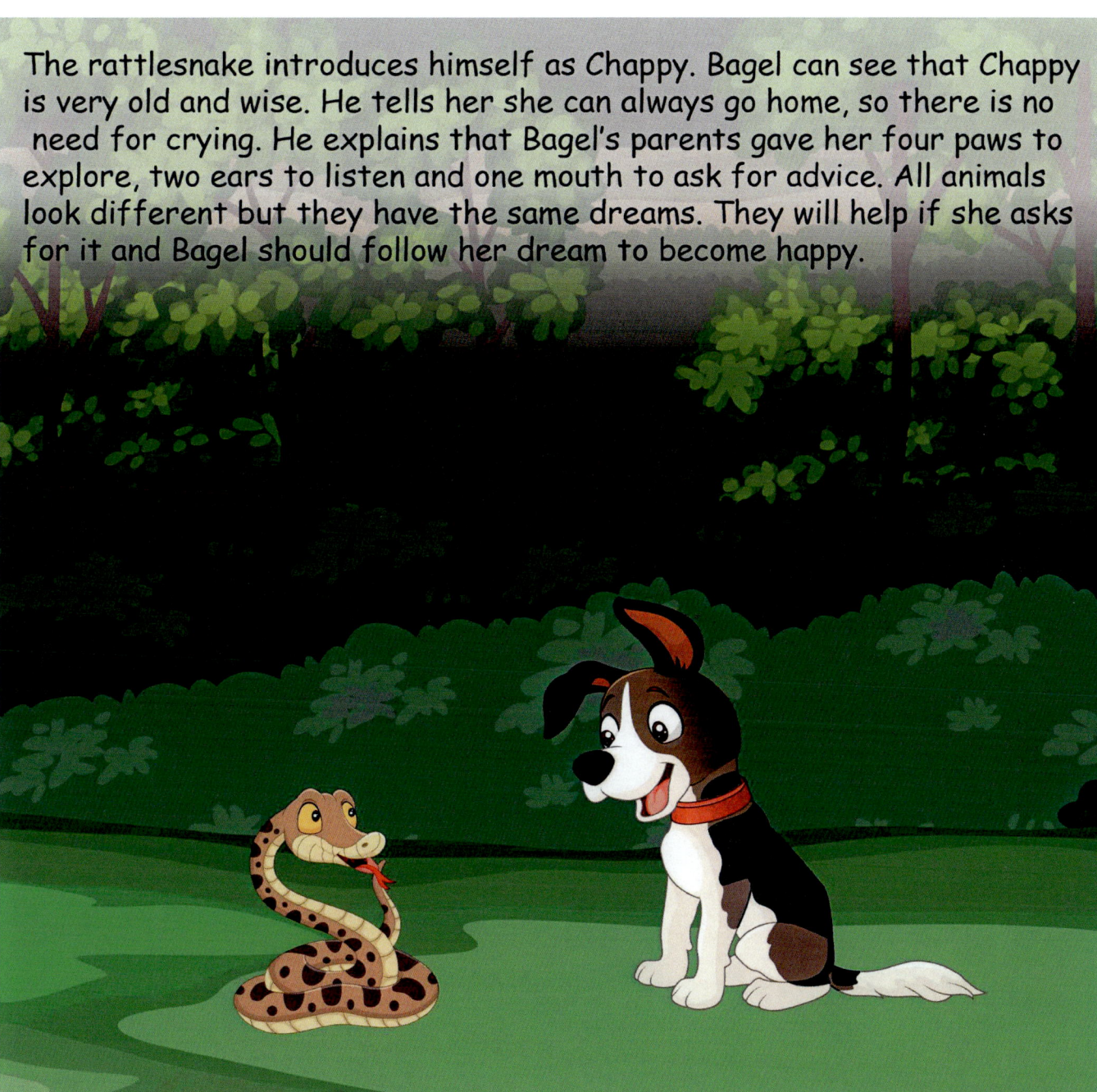

The next day Sally and Bagel arrive at the Colorado River in the Grand Canyon. The river is so big! How should they get across? Sally can't help and needs to get home to her girl friend.
Bagel sits and wonders...what did Chappy say???
Ask for help and they will help. but who to ask!

Suddenly she hears the wind picking up and it sounds like a storm. Bagel looks up and high in the sky sje sees a bald eagle. Bagel shouts "Hi Mister Baldy can you help me over the Grand Canyon. Pleeeeeeeaaase?"

Baldy the eagle lands next to Bagel and tells her "Yes of course, where are you off to my child?" Bagel explains she is off to California to see the blue ocean but she can't get over the Grand Canyon and she has traveled so far and is so tired.

Baldy laughs and says no problemo kiddo "I will take you. Jump on my back and hold on." Bagel is afraid to look down but does it anyway. They fly over Las Vegas and she has never seen so much light before. She will have to come back and take a closer look one day.
Chappy was right. People will help if you ask for it. She can see the entire world from Baldy's back. The world is truly amazing, and she knows she has to see it all.

Baldy takes her to Venice Beach. She is here, at the end of her journey. All she can see is sand and palm trees. All of a sudden, she hears the sound of waves just like the old mutt described and Bagel runs toward the sound. Then she finally sees the blue ocean. Her dream came true, she was right.

In the blue ocean she sees a big whale blow water, two dolphins surfing in the waves and pelicans catching fish. Bagel thinks it is the most beautiful thing she has ever seen. She is so happy and proud she trusted her dreams and followed them to the ocean.

The
🐾
End

Made in United States
North Haven, CT
26 August 2023

40765121R00020